Dear Judy.
Nearly a Boxer?
Happy Birthday 2015.
       Love

Annie and Peter.

D1429133

The Rascal

Episodes in the Life of a Bulldog Pup

The Rascal

Episodes in the Life of a Bulldog Pup

Pictured by
CECIL ALDIN

Edited by Roy Heron

Souvenir Press

First published in 1905 by William Heinemann as *A Gay Dog*.
Published in New York as *A Conceited Puppy*.

This edition © Souvenir Press 2009

This edition published in Great Britain in 2009 by Souvenir
Press Ltd
43 Great Russell Street, London WC1B 3PD

ISBN 9780285638600

Typeset and re-originated by MRM Graphics Ltd, Winslow,
Bucks

Printed and bound in Thailand under the supervision of
MRM Graphics Ltd

The Rascal

The Story of a Foolish Year

We were three in the litter. I inherited my beauty from my mother. My sisters took after father. At the show I was decorated with a red ribbon, which created no end of bad feeling. My sisters said some peculiarly nasty things on the subject of my nose, but I turned it up and smiled. He who laughs last, laughs best.

It may seem unbrotherly, but honestly, I was not sorry when we were parted. Attracted by my personal charms, a young man with a window in his eye carried me off in a hansom cab. My sisters looked gloomily on. Poor things! They would never know life as I was to know it.

Life in its real sense began for me when the youth with the window in his eye presented me to a lady friend of his.

Pammy was her name, and her business seemed to consist in changing her clothes, while I sat by and guarded the door from intruders.

After each change a boy called her loudly, and she rustled off, leaving me alone in her dressing room. The first time she did it I looked for the chocolates which our young man had brought us, but I found nothing but filthy pink and white paint, which stuck to my nose —

– and made me sick. I vowed revenge! It was Pammy who ate the chocolates.

My chance came when Pammy had a part for me written into the play she was acting. I was to rescue her from the swell villain, and at the rehearsals I did it to everyone's satisfaction. But on the night of the performance, I feigned stage- fright, and the whole scene was spoiled. Some dogs are too readily imposed upon – not I!

I have always upheld to the best of my ability the dignity of Doghood. At Ascot a beggar with a banjo kept shoving an evil-smelling butterfly net into my face.

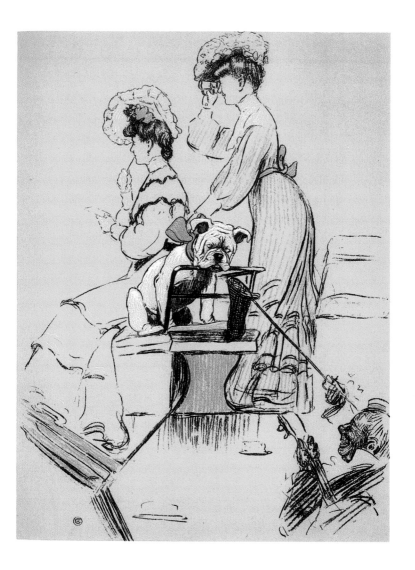

When I caught hold of it and started a sort of tug-of-war, a lot of money fell out. Then the beggar swore and Pammy seemed frightened, while all the roughs around scrambled for the money. I could not help laughing.

Pammy made up her mind that coaching and racing were not good for me. So we got a motor from our young man. But the roads were too dusty for me.

On the whole boating suited me best, and Henley Regatta was certainly the most enjoyable feature of my London season. But even that delightful reunion of the elite, as Pammy called it, was spoiled by human perversity. I was reaching over the punt end for a biscuit that was floating temptingly on the water –

– When a fool in a boat crashed into our punt and sent me flying into the river.

Pammy flew into a temper and would not let me go near her. I shrugged my shoulders and she screamed worse than ever.

Pride, however, had its fall, and Pammy's condition on our way to Ostend seemed a just retribution for her want of tenderness when I was in straits.

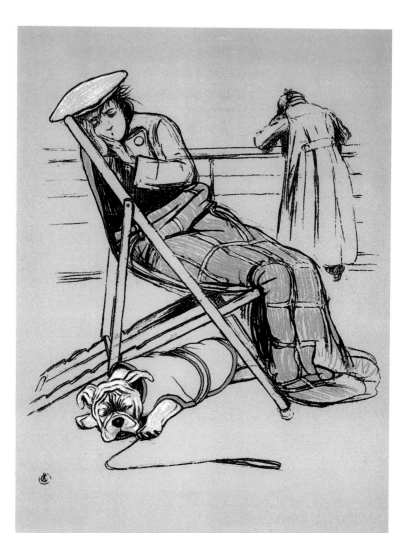

Next morning we discovered the most curious creatures on the sea- shore. Certainly the likes cannot be seen in our own tight little island. Pammy has no discretion, and she actually allowed one of these hairy savages to teach her how to swim.

I turned my attention to the local dog – a thing pitiable in its hideousness, and hairy in patches like its master.

I soon discovered that he was an empty-headed fop, and made him feel the superiority of British stamina.

When we returned to England we took lodgings at a farmhouse in the depths of the country. On the way Pammy wanted to bundle me off like a piece of luggage in the guard's van. "Not much," said I, "I'll go with you or stay in town." I travelled with her – first class. You must be firm with women.

When we arrived at our destination, her temper was as sour as mine was sweet. She'd been sleeping in the train, and I had the greatest difficulty to get her out of it.

Next morning Pam stayed in bed till mid-day, but I was up and about early, making important discoveries all over the place. Few Londoners know of the existence of the Comedian Bird. I came across a fine specimen that very day.

And I was surrounded by a chattering and protesting throng when I took my breakfast off a pan in the yard.

They were all good-natured enough, and I was encouraged to put my trust in the simple folk of the country side.

But strolling afield I came across a curious horned horse – spotty and clumsy. I went up unsuspectingly to make its acquaintance and addressed it as a well-bred dog should.

But a moment afterwards I found myself head over heels and out of the meadow.

I can't say that I have ever recovered from the shock!

Indeed, I am so poorly that Pammy has determined to leave me with the farmer. Of course, I shall never make friends and bring myself down to his level. I may find consolation in the rising generation and the "simple life," but my days as a devil-may-care rapscallion are over.

Also available from Souvenir Press

"One of my favourite books of all time... This adorable book is
enhanced by wonderful drawings by Cecil Aldin."
Jilly Cooper, 'Sunday Express'

A DOG DAY

Cecil Aldin

Told by Walter Emanuel

9780285635289   **£8.99**

Who can resist a dog who manages to wind the entire household around his paws
while committing sins that deserve the harshest punishment?

Greedy, always looking for unguarded food and ready to take revenge on the only
person in the house who doesn't like him, he remains utterly appealing. *A Dog Day*
remains Cecil Aldin's most enduring creation.

"Quite the best dog story ever written."
'Guardian'

Available from all good bookshops, Amazon.co.uk and Amazon.com.

"Classic old-style *Punch* comedy."
'The Countryman'

PUPPY DOGS' TALES

Cecil Aldin

Told by Roy Heron

9780285636569   **£8.99**

The illustrations for *Puppy Dogs' Tales* have been selected from the drawings, full of zest and humour, which Aldin drew for a series of books in the years before World War One.

The mischievous puppies of this book are Scamp, the mongrel; Poppy, named after her red colouring; Bob-tailed Bill, who has a truncated rear-end and Snowball, the white terrier.

"Has captivated generations and has that rare quality of appealing to young and old."
'All About Dogs'